GROLIER
B O O K S

After spending years in prison for puppy-napping, Cruella De Vil was free. She was now a changed woman. By undergoing a special treatment, she had learned to love dogs and *hate* furs!

Clutching her dog, Fluffy, Cruella ordered her assistant, Alonso, to gather up her furs and her Dalmatian puppy-coat design. Then she had him throw them into a secret room in her mansion.

"Lock them away! Bury them beyond sight and memory!" Cruella shouted to Alonso.

But had Cruella really changed?
Her probation officer, Chloe, didn't
think so. It was Chloe's job to check up
on the released prisoner.

Chloe's Dalmatians were upset, too,
when they learned Cruella was free. After
all, they had just welcomed three adorable
puppies into the world.

Chloe promised her dogs Dipstick and Dottie
that she'd be keeping her eye on Cruella.

Chloe and her dogs weren't the only ones with worries. Kevin, a young man who ran the Second Chance Dog Shelter, had worries, too. The shelter was closing because it had run out of money.

Kevin had several dogs of his own and a parrot named Waddlesworth. The bird wouldn't fly because he thought he was a dog!

"Don't worry, everything will be all right," Kevin told his pals. But he didn't know how to save the shelter.

Imagine Kevin's surprise
when Cruella arrived at
the shelter one day.
"This place and I were
made for each other,"
Cruella told Kevin.
She bought the
shelter on the spot!

Within days, Cruella had repaired and redecorated the entire shelter. She even came every day to groom the dogs.

Kevin was thrilled. But Chloe was suspicious and kept visiting the shelter to keep an eye on Cruella.

"People like Cruella don't change," Chloe told Kevin.

Time passed. Chloe's puppies grew
and got their spots, except for little Oddball,
who remained pure white.

But Oddball kept trying to get spots. One day
Chloe brought the puppies to her office. While trying
to get spots from a copier machine, little Oddball fell
out of a window.

At that moment, Chloe happened to be meeting
with Cruella. Suddenly Chloe looked up and saw
Oddball outside! Chloe quickly ran to the window
and hauled the puppy inside to safety.

Just then London's huge clock, Big Ben, began to
chime. It echoed though the open window.

BONG! BONG! BONG!

Unfortunately, Big Ben's chimes reversed the
treatment Cruella had undergone in prison. Strange
things started happening. An odd smile twisted her
mouth. Her hair stood on end. Spots danced before
her eyes. The evil, fur-loving Cruella was back!

Cruella raced home. She tore open her secret
room and grabbed her Dalmatian puppy-coat design.
"My Dalmatian puppy coat. The coat of dreams!
The ultimate fur coat!" Cruella shrieked. "Alonso!
We're going to make them pay!" She would have
her coat at last and punish those who had put her
in prison for so long.

Cruella dashed off to see the famous fur fashion designer, Jean-Pierre LePelt. She showed him her coat design. They agreed that 102 puppies would be just the right number for her gorgeous, *hooded* Dalmatian puppy coat.

Cruella immediately set her evil plans in motion.
First, she had Alonso steal puppies from all over town.
She told him to hide some of the stolen Dalmatians at
the Second Chance Shelter. Then Cruella called the
police to have Kevin arrested for puppy-napping.

While Chloe looked on in shock, Kevin protested.
"This is crazy!" he said. "Why would I steal
Dalmatians?"

But the police took Kevin and his pets to jail.

Next, Cruella told LePelt to steal Chloe's puppies. She invited Chloe and Dipstick to a party to keep them out of the way.

Chloe and her dog arrived at Cruella's mansion. Other guests had also brought their dogs, and dinner quickly got out of hand. Dogs started to climb on tables, step on plates, and splatter food on everyone.

In the middle of everything, Cruella's dog, Fluffy, barked timidly. He wanted to warn Dipstick and Chloe of Cruella's plans. The pair followed him to the secret fur room.

Chloe peeked inside the room and gasped when she saw the fur-coat design. "The puppy coat!" cried Chloe. Her puppies were in danger.

Just then Cruella appeared. "Good-bye, my dear!" Cruella hissed. She shoved Chloe into the room and locked the door.

Dipstick managed to get away. While Fluffy worked to free Chloe, Dipstick rushed home to save his family.

Back at Chloe's, LePelt was chasing Dottie and
the puppies from room to room. He smashed chairs,
scattered books, and broke lamps. As the designer
reached for Oddball, she darted to a window and
barked for help. LePelt finally grabbed the puppy and
stuffed her into his bag. But another puppy nearby
had heard her yelps for help.

Bark by bark, Oddball's call was passed from puppy to puppy. The Twilight Bark echoed across London.

Kevin's parrot, Waddlesworth, heard it in jail. He understood that Chloe's puppies needed help. So he took the keys from a sleeping guard and freed Kevin and the dogs. Together they raced towards Chloe's home.

Dipstick had also heard the Twilight
Bark. This made him run even faster.

Chloe and Kevin reached Chloe's home at the same time. The mess was terrible. But worst of all, Dottie and the puppies had been stolen!

"How will we ever find them?" Chloe thought.

Kevin's dogs pawed through the debris. Finally, with an excited WOOF, they uncovered a train ticket. It was LePelt's.

"Paris–the Orient Express at ten," Chloe cried, looking at the ticket. "We can just make it."

Meanwhile, Dipstick was almost home when he heard familiar barking coming from a truck. Dipstick knew it was his family! He quickly leapt onto the truck.

The truck stopped at an alley outside the train station. When the truck's door opened, Dipstick lunged. He landed in Alonso's arms. But after a struggle, Alonso managed to shove Dipstick into a crate.

Cruella was taking the puppies by train to LePelt's workshop in Paris. But when she pulled Oddball from the bag, Cruella dropped the white puppy.

"A rat!" Cruella shouted. "I asked for spotted dogs!"

Oddball scampered off into the train station.

"Find that dog and get rid of it!" Cruella screamed at Alonso.

Racing through the station, Oddball dodged
suitcases and ducked past feet. Alonso puffed
after her. Finally he gave up and boarded the train
to join Cruella and LePelt. His truck, Cruella's
car, and all the dogs were already aboard.

"You took care of the rat?" Cruella asked him.

"You will never see it again," Alonso replied.

The train began to move. Oddball ran
after it, trying to jump aboard. Just then,
Chloe, Kevin and his pets arrived and saw
Oddball on the tracks.

"She'll be killed" Chloe cried out. It was then that
Waddlesworth flew for the first time in his life! The
bird snatched up Oddball and landed inside the train
with a *THUMP*.

Waddlesworth and Oddball found Cruella's car on
the train. They both hid inside it, not knowing what
to do next.

The train rumbled on through the night. Once in Paris, Cruella and LePelt drove to LePelt's workshop in her car. Alonso took the dogs along in his truck.

As they rode along, the puppies barked the Twilight Bark to the dogs of Paris. Soon Chloe, Kevin and his pets arrived in Paris, too. The Parisian dogs led them straight to LePelt's workshop.

Meanwhile, Waddlesworth and Oddball had slipped into the workshop unnoticed by the workers. The noise of the worker's sewing machines filled the room. Luckily, Oddball could hear the other dogs in the cellar. But how would they ever get them out?

Waddlesworth noticed a hole in the floor. If he could just make it larger, he decided, the puppies could escape through it. The parrot began to bite the soft wood with his sharp beak.

When Kevin and Chloe reached
LePelt's workshop, they sneaked
into the cellar through a trap door.
Their pets greeted them joyfully.
But then Cruella poked her
head through the trap door.

"Aren't you in a tight spot!"
she cackled as she slammed
the door shut. The lock turned.
Now everyone was trapped—
well, almost everyone.

At that moment, Waddlesworth stuck his beak
through the hole he had chewed.

"Psst, up here!" the parrot whispered.

Working swiftly, Chloe and Kevin began
passing the puppies up through the hole in the floor.

Upstairs, Oddball led the puppies to a door. It was
locked! Desperately looking for another way out, she
headed up a staircase. One by one, the puppies
climbed the creaking stairs. It seemed as if they
might get away when Cruella spotted them.

"It's the little rat!" Cruella screamed when she saw
Oddball. Then she turned towards Alonso. "You lied to
me! You worm!" She raced after the puppies.

"You *are* a wormy little man!" LePelt agreed.
Alonso had had enough! He wanted to help the dogs.

Alonso tackled the fashion designer. Back and forth the two men wrestled until—WHUMPF! Alonso had the arms of LePelt's coat stitched together by one of the workers—with LePelt in it! The designer stumbled and fell through the hole Waddlesworth had made in the floor. LePelt was stuck in the hole!

Alonso rushed to the trap door. He opened it and set Kevin, Chloe, and the rest of the dogs free.

In the meantime, Cruella was still chasing the puppies. She followed them up the stairs, across the attic, and out of a window. Oddball urged the puppies across a narrow bridge to the bakery next door. Cruella tore after them.

"This time, it's personal!" she screamed.

Inside the bakery, the puppies dashed
to safety as Oddball tried to hold off
Cruella. But Cruella wouldn't be stopped.
Grabbing a cable, she swung across the room,
accidentally hitting a button with her foot.

CLANK, CLANK! The baking machinery
came to life.

Cruella lost her grip on the cable and fell into a huge mixing bowl of cake batter.

The giant mixing bowl moved along a conveyor belt.

"Aaagh!" Cruella yelled as eggs splattered down upon on her head.

"Blech! Glub!" Cruella sputtered as she was covered with flour and milk.

Round and round the mixing bowl turned. It churned Cruella into a mass of gloopy, gluey dough! Then it tipped over and poured "Cruella goo" into a huge cake pan. The cake was ready for baking . . . .

By now Chloe and Kevin had arrived. Yapping joyfully, the dogs and their friends were reunited. Not long after—DING!—the oven door opened and the cake came out—with a crusty Cruella in the middle!

Jumping on tubes of icing, the puppies decorated the Cruella cake. What fun!

Outside the bakery, the Paris police were waiting to take a crumbly Cruella off to jail once again. LePelt was unstuck from the hole and arrested, too.

Everyone else was soon back in London.

A few weeks later, Alonso and Fluffy showed up at the Second Chance Shelter with a big surprise. "I asked if I could have the pleasure of delivering this," Alonso began. Cruella had been forced to give her entire fortune to the dogs! "Judge's orders," Alonso added. Everyone cheered. The dogs would be safe now.

But little Oddball barked the loudest. Everyone looked up to see her sitting happily in the dog sculpture at the front of the shelter. Soon they could see why she was so happy. The brave little puppy's fur was no longer pure white. Oddball had gotten her spots at last!